Magenta and Me!

by Deborah Reber
illustrated by Don Bishop

Ready-to-Read

Simon Spotlight/Nick Jr.

New York   London   Toronto   Sydney   Singapore

NOTE TO PARENTS

Welcome to the series of Ready-to-Read books done the Blue's Clues way! This line of books has been researched to ensure a high level of interactivity in this simple rebus format. Children are encouraged to read along by reading the pictures above the words in this story. Because the word is also underneath each picture, your child will begin to recognize and learn each word as well!

To Anne Marie Kane . . . my "Magenta"—D. R.
To my little Blue's fans, Kevin and Ryan—D. B.

Based on the TV series *Blue's Clues*® created by Traci Paige Johnson, Todd Kessler, and Angela C. Santomero as seen on Nick Jr.®
On *Blue's Clues,* Steve is played by Steven Burns.

SIMON SPOTLIGHT
An imprint of Simon & Schuster Children's Publishing Division
1230 Avenue of the Americas, New York, New York 10020

Manufactured in the United States of America
8 10 9

Library of Congress Cataloging-in-Publication Data
Reber, Deborah.
Magenta and me / by Deborah Reber ; illustrated by Don Bishop.—1st ed.
p. cm. — (Ready-to-read)
"#2."
Based on the TV series Blues clues created by Traci Paige Johnson, Todd Kessler,
and Angela C. Santomero.
Summary: From helping each other at school to sharing a special play date, Blue and Magenta do lots of fun things together as best friends. Features rebuses.
ISBN 0-689-83123-4 (pbk.)
1. Rebuses. [1. Blue—Fiction. 2. Best friends—Fiction. 3. Dogs—Fiction. 4. Stories in rhyme.
5. Rebuses.]
I. Bishop, Don, ill. II. Title. III. Series.
PZ8.3.R24435 Mag 2000
[Fic]—dc21
99-46900

Hi, it's me, !
BLUE
And this is my best
friend, !
MAGENTA

3

MAGENTA has SPOTS and big
ears just like me!

4

But she's  MAGENTA and I'm BLUE, so we're different, you see?

5

and I met on

MAGENTA

our first day of .

SCHOOL

6

We were both a little shy, but  SCHOOL was so cool!

Now we see each other at  SCHOOL almost every day.

We read  BOOKS , paint PICTURES , and take time to play!

9

When  reads
MISS MARIGOLD

, we sit together
BOOKS

on the reading ◯.
RUG

10

And when it's time to say good-bye, we give each other a .

HUG

Some days  comes

MAGENTA

over to play after [image of schoolhouse].

SCHOOL

12

Then we play in the  SANDTABLE or swim in my POOL.

13

Other times we
try to find
in the .

BIRDS

TREES

Then we make
a  of the
LIST   BIRDS
we see.

15

If it's  we play
RAINING
different games in
my  .

ROOM

Like marching parade with my 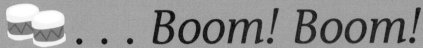. . . Boom! Boom! Boom!

DRUMS

MAGENTA is so silly, she's always making me things.

18

She made me this ⭕ out of 🍜 and 〰️.

BRACELET NOODLES STRING

She also drew this  that I hung on my wall.

PICTURE

knew that my favorite season was fall.

Look, I'm making a  for today.

PRESENT   MAGENTA

22

It's a big "M" for

MAGENTA

that I made out

of 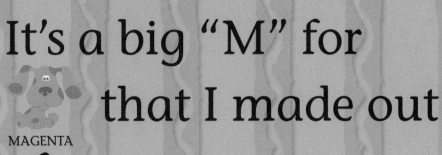 .

CLAY

And here is my  CARD

that I'm ready to

send: